WELCOME

to

HELL

Kristen Houghton

WELCOME TO HELL

by Kristen Houghton

© Copyright 2017 by Kristen Houghton. All rights reserved

ISBN-13: 978-1-7324166-1-1

Library of Congress Cataloguing-in-Publication Data Houghton, Kristen

WELCOME TO HELL 1st. ed.

1. Teddy Jameson (Fictitious character)-Fiction 2. fantasy 3. horror 4. humor noir 5. The Devil 6. Hell

Published by **Skylight-NYC Publishers**, LLC 175 Fifth Avenue New York, NY, 10010

Skylight-NYCPublishers.com skylight-nyc@outlook.com

Cover by 2Hopper Production & Design Studio

DEDICATION

To all of us who have been blessed, or cursed, with an imagination…and to the memory of the incredibly talented Rod Sterling whose *Twilight Zone* stories thrilled me, scared me, and made my imagination soar.

CONTENTS

BOOKS BY KRISTEN HOUGHTON

CRIME AND MYSTERY

CATE HARLOW PRIVATE INVESTIGATION SERIES

Sins of the Fathers

Grave Misgivings

Unrepentant: Pray for Us Sinners

FANTASY

THE TEDDY JAMESON CHRONICLES

Leaving Hell with the Angel of Redemption 2019

HISTORICAL ROMANCE

The Anchoress: A Romantic Tale of Terror

ANTHOLOGY

No Woman Diets Alone-There's Always a Man Behind Her Eating a Doughnut

And Then I'll Be Happy! Stop Sabotaging Your Happiness and Put Your Own Life First

YOUNG ADULT NOVELLA

Remember, Hetty?

COMING IN 2019

Lilith Angel, a YA fantasy series

ACKNOWLEDGMENTS

To 2Hopper Design Studio for the in-depth cover artwork
To KH Koehler, friend and author, whose expertise and guidance in all
areas of "book work" inspires me, and to author and friend Carole Nelson
Douglas, who told me that I could.

WELCOME TO HELL

"**M**R. JAMESON? MR. *JAMESON?* SIR? Hell-*ooooo!* Mr. Jame—ah, you've come around I see, you're *here.*"

A nude and startled Teddy Jameson opened his eyes and looked around, dazed.

"*Here?* What's 'here'? Where the hell am I?"

"Oh ho, funny, very funny, indeed, Mr. Jameson!"

"I'm sorry? Funny? About what? I don't—"

"Yes, most likely you *don't.* Well—I hope your journey wasn't too uncomfortable. We like to save *that* for later! You get it Mr. Jameson? Oh, probably not; it's a little inside joke, oh well." The man laughed quietly and coughed. "Here are your clothes; mustn't be naked, not yet! Now then. Ahem! Mr. Theodore Carter Hugh Jameson, may I be the first to welcome you to Hell. Now if you'll just follow me."

Ted looked around him and was, his guide was happy to see, totally amazed. Teddy looked at the man, standing next to him and was amazed all over again. The man resembled a gay version of Brad Pitt!

"Are we surprised, Mr. Jameson? Pleasantly so, I think, right? Am I right? Ah, yes, I believe I am!"

"Wait! Did you say hell as in capital 'H,' as in a *noun* type of word, as in a *place? The* Hell?"

"*The* one and only, Mr. Jameson."

"But I'm not dead! I was just, I was just, uh, I—"

"Were just humping and pumping your girlfriend, I know. But you *are* dead and you *are* in the one and only Hell. You keeled over from a brain aneurysm, the kind from which they were able to save Sharon Stone. Of course *she* had the sense to go to the hospital when she got a splitting headache, but not *you.* No, you thought it would go away after you smoked a joint and banged your sweetie's pie but, oops, no, didn't work, did it? Instead it killed you!"

"How can this be Hell when it looks like a vacation at Sandals Resorts and how come the devil looks like a faggy Brad Pitt?"

"Oh, how very nice of you! You really think *I'm* the Devil?! I am so flattered! Oh my goodness, oh that is good, oh Hell's bells, but no-o, no, no, no. *The* Devil doesn't have time to meet and greet just anyone and besides, he is *the* Devil, so please, why would he be bothered doing menial work? No, no, I'm just one of his demons, an upper class one to be sure, but still, just a demon."

"Okay listen, you look like the actor my girlfriend would love to have between her legs, this place looks like a Caribbean vacation spot, and, by the way, where the fuck is your pointed tail and horns or whatever, if you're a real demon?" Teddy finished putting on his clothes and zipped up.

"Oh, Mr. Jameson! What lovely, lovely language! But seriously, fashions do change, even here! We no longer wear the horns or tails, oh, no! They are so passé! So Medieval! And this place? Well, it did need an upgrade. I mean, it is old as, well, as old as Hell. Ha, ha! That's another inside joke, Mr. Jameson."

"You know my name, what's yours? *Brad?*" His guide looked startled. "That's my inside joke."

"It's Wallis if you must know." The pseudo-Brad Pitt looked down timidly.

"Wallis?! *Wa*llis. Well, Wally, I have a feeling that this is an elaborate joke on the part of my buddies who slipped some fucking hallucinogen into that joint and hired you to play the devil or his henchman or whoever. I am, as those whack-jobs back in the sixties used to say, 'having a trip'. Now if you could just let me sleep it off, I promise I'll pay you triple what those bastards said they would. I'm good for the money. Deal, Wally-Wally Bing Bang?"

"Mr. Jameson, I am afraid that you don't under—"

"No, Wally, *you* don't understand. I've got an early morning tennis game with this bitch department chair who can make or break my academic career. And I'm going to make sure my career is as nicely made as a high priced French whore's silk-sheeted bed. And speaking of beds, can you direct me to a bedroom? *Please?* I want to lie down."

"But Mr. Jameson, no one hired me to play anyone! I could never, ever, presume to impersonate His Highness, never!"

"Look, Wally? I'm pretty pissed right now and I don't want to kick the shit out of you just because you happen to be the hapless schmuck who my buddies are paying to pull off this sick trick, but punching you in the head is starting to seem to me like the best idea right now."

Wallis stood his ground without flinching. "I really think, sir, that you might want, at the very least, to ask me some questions. Aren't you even the slightest bit curious? Why don't you sit down on that bench over there and we'll talk, shall we?"

Teddy sighed, walked over to the elaborately carved bench and sat down. Wallis stood in front of him. "Okay, Walls, you got me. I do have questions, just two, actually. Number one: Which one of my dear, head-case friends approached you to pull this scam on me and exactly how much are they paying you? Question two: Was my girlfriend, Mitzy involved in this because she didn't smoke any weed and the girl loves her weed. You think you can answer those simple little questions, Wally my man?"

"The one about your girlfriend, yes, I can answer that one. She didn't smoke because she just had a Botox treatment today and she was afraid of mixing the two. She's a bit stupid if you ask me, but there it is. But, as to your friends, I must tell you again, *no one* is paying me *anything*. You *are* dead and you most certainly *are* in Hell."

"That's it, Wally!"

Teddy Jameson jumped up and went to put his hands around Wallis's throat but before he could connect he heard a voice behind him say, "Is everything all right Wallis?"

"Oh my Lord! Yes, yes, everything is fine, I believe."

Ted turned to find a tanned, blonde-haired man in tennis whites looking at Wallis with concern. It was hard to judge the man's age because he looked fit and athletic. His hair was surfer blonde as if, besides playing tennis, he spent a lot of time on the beach. His eyes were a greenish blue and he was what most women would call hot. If Teddy had to guess, he'd say the man was somewhere in his fifties, but extremely well-preserved. His presence had an immediate effect on Wallis.

"Oh I am so sorry you were disturbed! I cannot believe I allowed this to happen." He walked over to the tennis man and, falling to his knees, kissed one of the man's immaculately white sneakers.

"Stop groveling, Wallis," the man said quietly as he stepped backward. Wallis immediately got to his feet and bowed, then stood there, anxiously waiting.

"Go find something to do. I want to be alone with Mr. Jameson. Go now, Wallis." And Wallis went, tripping over his own feet, his demeanor that of a naughty puppy.

"Hello, Mr. Jameson. How are you?" The man's voice was smooth and mellow, almost sweet, if you could call a distinctly masculine voice sweet. "Shake hands with the Devil."

He smiled and held out his hand and Teddy shook it. The hand was warm and dry, the grip firm but not punishing. Teddy looked at the man and started to laugh.

"The Devil?! Of course! I get it! Irish Bernie! Now I know which one of my sick friends put you guys up to this charade. Bernie O'Connell, that prick! Always jealous of me and now I'm in line to get a full professorship he wants to fuck me over good. He knows I have to make a good impression tomorrow. That line you just said? That gave it away. His Irish mick of a father used to say that to me all the time when I was a kid. 'Shake hands with the devil, lad!' Oh man, I should've guessed. That bastard Bernie! When I'm done flying from this trip, I'm gonna kick his druggie ass!"

The man smiled, his eyes crinkling up nicely. "Shall we walk a bit, Mr. Jameson? It's a pleasant day for a walk."

Teddy smiled back, stood up and walked with him. "So. I know Wally's name. What's yours, if I may ask? Do you guys do this for a living or what? Go and mess with people's minds for a fee?"

"I'm Mr. Bello and I guess you could say this *is* a job. A very interesting one. We're certainly never bored.

"Yeah, I bet. What do you charge for this? I have to say that it's pretty damn good. Must be expensive with all this." He indicated the resort and the view. Mr. Bello smiled again.

"The price *is* high, Mr. Jameson, but business has never been better. Dirty tricks and scams are very popular among our clientele and we are paid rather—well."

"The wages of sin, huh? I mean, you and your group make a profit on this stuff, right?"

"You might say that. By the way, how's your headache, Mr. Jameson, has it gone away?"

Mr. Bello looked very solicitous. Teddy stopped walking and looked at Mr. Bello. His headache was gone, his head felt fine. In fact, *he* felt fine. None of the heart pounding after-effects he usually had from smoking pot. He was a little warm but otherwise fine, great in fact.

"Yeah, I'm fine, great. Hey, what the hell was in that joint? Something that makes a person wake up clear-headed and refreshed?" Mr. Bello laughed softly.

"Boy, I think I've just found you another way to make money!" Teddy wiped his face. "Hey, mind if we sit awhile? I'm starting to sweat like a pig."

"Of course, Mr. Jameson. We'll sit over there by the pool in one of those loungers."

"This place must be expensive to rent," Teddy said absent-mindedly.

"Actually I own it. It was—given to me by a former employer. A parting gift you might call it.

"Wow! You must've been important. What did you do? Law, corporate?"

"A combination of both, Mr. Jameson."

"My Dad told me to go into law but my mother said I'd be selling my soul if I did."

Mr. Bello laughed, showing perfect white teeth. Teddy wiped his hand across his face. It was hot and getting hotter. He looked at Mr. Bello who stood there looking like he'd stepped out of *Gentleman's Quarterly* mag. Not one bead of sweat. He looked perfect. Teddy found himself thinking that if he himself weren't heterosexual, he might find Mr. Bello attractive! Shit!

"You know, since I'm probably going to require your services to get even with that fuck Bernie, I think we should be on a first name basis. You can call me Teddy and I can call you—?"

"I prefer we call each by our surnames, if you don't mind, Mr. Jameson. It keeps everything a bit more—professional."

Teddy was taken aback. It was so common today to call even perfect strangers by their first names. Twenty-year old bank clerks thought nothing of calling eighty-five year customers by their first names. "Okay, well, if you prefer it that way."

Teddy sighed deeply. He was dripping with sweat. "Now my job, well, I'm an economics prof and I need to make a damned good impression on my chairperson come the morning. Got to think about how I can advance myself in her eyes, you know what I mean?"

"I wouldn't worry about your job, Mr. Jameson. That's not something you should be concerned about—now."

"Easy for you to say. You must have made quite an impression on your old boss to get this set-up here! By the way, if you don't mind my asking, where the hell is 'here?'"

"Don't you know Mr. Jameson? Can't you guess?"

"The Bahamas?"

"Guess again, Mr. Jameson." Mr. Bello looked at his watch, a top of the line Rolex if Teddy knew anything about watches. GQ all the way.

"Okay, then its Bermuda or Jamaica or any of those islands that Mitzy likes which are hot as hell. We're in the Caribbean, though, right?"

"How's your wife Catherine, Mr. Jameson?"

"What?" Teddy felt the heat rise in his face.

"Was she well the last time you saw her? You know, before you took off for your, let me be crude here, your whore's townhouse?" Mr. Bello's voice was still smooth and honey-rich even as he said the word 'whore.'

Anger fueled him. Teddy tried to get up too fast and a sudden wave of dizziness took over. He swayed forward and Mr. Bello deftly caught him, then eased him back down, gently, in the lounge chair. It was so fucking hot!

"Who *are* you? Where the hell am I?"

"I think you know the answer to both questions, Mr. Jameson. Think about it. Think hard."

"Look, whatever Bernie is paying you, I'll triple it. This isn't a joke anymore. He's always envied me, always—in college, my marriage, and now my new job. Hates me for making a decent life for myself but, shit, he blew his own life with drugs and booze. Why is he fucking around with mine?" Teddy stopped, then, "Am I being blackmailed by that bastard? Is he threatening to tell my wife about Mitzy? What about my employer? Are you taping me or what?"

"Care for a tennis match, Mr. Jameson? I understand that you're quite

15

a good player."

"In this fucking heat? I only play in the early morning hours before it gets too hot. What are you crazy? It must be two hundred degrees out! I hate playing tennis in the heat!"

Mr. Bello laughed and murmured, "Tennis in the heat. Do you want some water? Let me get you some water. Yes, Mr. Jameson? Some cold water?"

Before Teddy could answer an old man, with his head bent down, slowly walked over and put a glass of water on the table. Even though he couldn't see his face Teddy felt there was something oddly familiar about the man. He drank the water down in one gulp and sat shaking his head. Bello walked over to the man and Teddy heard him say, "Check the food preparation for the dinner gala, but remember, do not eat anything. You understand what will happen if you do."

The old man nodded and for a brief second looked at Teddy with a sad smile.

"Something the matter, Mr. Jameson?"

"That man. He—I think I might know him. I—Damn it! What did Bernie have you do to me? It's so God-damned hot!"

"Ah, yes, Mr. Jameson. It is *God-damned* hot, yes, it is. That it is! Any hint of where you might be then? Still haven't figured it out? Don't you know who that man is?"

Teddy just looked at him, confused.

"Teddy Jameson, Professor of Economics, bright, young man, with a pretty wife, and a pretty mistress, everyone says you were sure to go places, oh if they only knew where! Ah, Mr. Jameson, you're a prize, a gem, actually!"

"What's going on here? I mean I know that this is a sadistic joke, but I get it all right? It can stop now. I would like to leave, and I mean *now*. I'll even pay you if that's what you want. You can double dip— money from Bernie, money from me. You'll make out really well. But let's end this right now. We're done here."

"Oh we're hardly done, Mr. Jameson. In fact, we've only just started. Won't you reconsider playing a quick game of tennis? I do so love the game. I haven't had a good young opponent until you came. You're good, very good. You were trained by the best, weren't you? Your father's brother, your Uncle Charles, a Wimbledon seed. You loved him more than your own father."

Teddy stared at him.

"Of course he treated you better than your real father ever did. Always looked out for you, kept your father from beating the shit out of you on many occasions. Slipped you a little money when he knew you wanted something all the other boys had and that penny-pinching old man of yours wouldn't get for you. Good ol' Uncle Charlie."

"Bernie really filled you in on my life, huh?"

"Have you seen your beloved uncle lately? How is he?"

"You fuck! If you know so much about my life, then you know that my uncle died twelve years ago."

"But have you *seen* him?"

"You are fucking crazy!" said Teddy through gritted teeth. Mr. Bello calmly checked his watch and looked at the horizon.

"Mr. Jameson, there are rules in life. Some get broken."

Teddy ignored that remark. What rules was he talking about anyway? Instead he asked, "Are there any other people here in paradise besides you, me, and Wally?" He saw Mr. Bello smile. "Oops, my-bad as my students would say, I forgot the old waiter. Hey, isn't he just a little too old to be playing at butler? I mean, this job just might kill him."

Mr. Bello threw his head back and laughed.

"Yeah, funny. So, are we waiting for old Bernz-a-matic to show up and revel at my predicament? Is the fuck going to blackmail me? Is that it?"

"Rules, Mr. Jameson, rules. Ah, yes."

Teddy looked at the sky. Two grey clouds in a sky so blue it hurt his eyes. Rain clouds, please let them be rain clouds. Once they burst, this place will cool off. He took a deep breath. It was suffocatingly hot! He got up and began to walk around the pool. Mr. Bello just watched him and kept checking his Rolex.

I'll kill Bernie, I'll run his drunken ass over with my car and say it was an accident. I'll poison his fucking liquor. Oh, God! What am I going to do if he tells my wife about Mitzy? What am I going to do if the university hears about it? My department chair is so damned tight-assed about faculty morals she needs an enema just to call the university president by his first name, which just happens to be Dick!

Teddy's thoughts went wild. This was insane. There had to be a way out. This guy, this Mr. Bello, he was nuts. He probably enjoyed driving people crazy. Got off that way. Bello, Bello—wait a minute that's an Italian name! Is he with the Mafia or what's left of the Mafia? Oh God! What's going on here? I don't want to stereotype people. I know there are Italians who have nothing to do with the mob, but, fuck! The mob's still alive and well! Who knows?

He saw the old man who had brought him the water and called out, "Hey, hey buddy! Mister! Over here! I gotta ask you something."

But the old man put his head down and kept walking, ambling away from Teddy in a slow shuffle.

"God!" yelled Teddy in frustration. "God damn, God damn, God damn. God damn you all!"

"Shhh! Mr. Jameson. Be quiet! Please be quiet!" It was Wallis hurrying over to him, finger on lips.

"Wally! What's going on? Is that prick Bernie trying to ruin my career and my marriage? Did he hire you to do that? Is this the fucking Mafia? Answer me! For God's sake, answer me! God, God, God!!!!"

"Shhh, shushhhhh! Please!! Don't say that! Please Mr. Jameson. Not here. Please, let's just walk a bit. I'm on my way to the beach, walk with me to the beach. Near the endless ocean, ha-ha, yes, we'll do that, right now."

Wallis took Teddy's arm and directed him towards the shore. The sand was so hot Teddy could feel it through his shoes. His clothes were sticking to him. Teddy was about to say something else when he noticed a small group of people on a boat out on the water.

A man and a woman were sitting in the prow. Suddenly the man stood up and roughly took the woman in his arms. She struggled, kicking and hitting at the man but he lifted her up and threw her over the side, into the water. From her horrified screams, it was obvious that she couldn't swim. She floundered and Teddy could hear gurgled calls for help. The other passengers sat in the boat ignoring her screams. He saw her go under, come up, and then go down again.

"Hey! That woman! She's drowning," yelled Teddy running to the water's edge. He pulled off his shoes and felt the sand sear his feet like grilled meat.

"No, wait Mr. Jameson! Wait!"

Wallis tried to grab him, but Teddy was too fast for him. The same legs that had helped him win many tennis matches stood him in good stead as he raced into the water. He swam towards the boat, his heart pounding with the strain and the horrible fact that he had possibly witnessed a crime. No one in the boat moved, they just watched silently as Teddy swam towards the spot where the woman had gone down.

Nearing the boat, he dove again and again, frantically searching. His lungs felt as if they were about to burst from the effort of holding his breath. He finally found her, floating just a few feet from where she had gone under. Grabbing an arm, he pulled her over to the side of the boat, signaling for help, but no one moved.

"Hey! Hey? A little help here, how about it people?"

They looked at the scene with detachment, as if they were watching a boring movie. Struggling with her dead weight, Teddy grabbed the side of the boat and gasped for breath. She was dead. Teddy knew it. No movement, no sign of life.

The man who had thrown her overboard slowly reached down and pulled her up over the side. He placed her in the bottom of the boat where she lay lifeless. Looking at the others in the boat, he said tonelessly, "She's dead. Died drowning. She was always terrified of drowning." Turning to Teddy, he gestured towards the beach. "You shouldn't have touched her.

You can go back to shore. We don't need you here."

He pushed at Teddy's head with an oar. Teddy was sputtering with disbelief and exhaustion. "*I* shouldn't have touched her?! You threw her overboard! I believe you've just committed a murder, you bastard! You killed a woman—she didn't die, she was murdered!" He pointed at the other passengers. "You all saw it happen and you did nothing. You bastards are fucking accomplices."

They stared ahead as if drugged.

"Go back to shore. We don't need you," the man repeated. He slapped at Teddy with an oar and this time hit his arm hard.

Teddy paddled backwards out of his way. I'm dealing with lunatics, he thought as he turned for the swim back. I've got to tell someone, get some help! Shit! Did someone pay Bello to have a person *killed*? Took a, what the hell is it called? a contract out on that woman? No, no I can't think that way. I can't believe he does that. If I do, then I can believe that he is capable of killing me!

Teddy looked back over his shoulder at the passengers in the boat. They were all staring off into the horizon the same as before. And then he saw an amazing sight. The dead woman raised her head, shook herself like a wet dog, and moved to the prow of the boat again. She wasn't drowned, she was alive! Teddy, treading water, started to shout something, but what he saw next stopped him cold. The same man who had thrown her overboard, approached again, took her into his arms and, just as before, threw her over the side of the boat! Her screams were terrible to hear.

Teddy watched, debating whether he should go back to try to save her from a guy who definitely wanted her dead. He was a strong swimmer, maybe he could try to get her to shore. But he decided that the boat would overtake them and that his interference might make the guy with the oar try to kill him too! Teddy swam back alone.

On shore he remembered the burning hot sand and was relieved to see his shoes being buffeted by the waves, just at the water's edge. He reached for them and slipped them on, wet feet or not. Wallis was waiting on the sand, his hands nervously clasped in front of him, almost as if he were praying.

"What the fuck is going on here, Wally? You guys into murder for hire?"

But Wally was staring out at the ocean and when Teddy turned in the direction Wallis was looking, he was hit with another shock. The woman's body was being pulled into the boat again by the same man who had thrown her overboard! She wasn't moving.

"This is murder, Wally, out and out murder. I'm a witness. And you are too. We have to contact the authorities. Listen, you don't have to be afraid of Bello, just show me how to get off the damn resort and we'll go get help. Did you know that Bello was into this? I mean, did you know that he was a hit man? Wally?" He grabbed him to get his attention, but Wallis shook free and kept staring out to where the boat was bobbing on the water.

"Twenty-three, come on make it twenty-three," Wallis kept saying. "Twenty-three, twenty-three, twenty......ah!"

Teddy followed Wallis' gaze and saw the 'dead' woman rise up again, shake her head, and go to the prow of the boat. After a few seconds the man grabbed her and threw her over the side. Her screams echoed across the short distance to the shore. Teddy watched in stunned amazement as the scene was re-enacted over and over again.

"Twenty-four, twenty-four," Wallis was chanting.

"Uh, Walls? Hey! What are you muttering about numbers? Please, okay? Please tell me what is going on!"

Screams, splash. Dead.

Rescued. Not dead.

"Yes! Ah, yes, yes!" Wallis was breathing heavily.

"Okay. This is just plain weird. Something, I don't know what, but something is happening here. Maybe murder, I don't know, but I have never—"

Scream, splash. Dead.

Rescued. Not dead.

"Twenty-five!! It's okay, okay. Twenty-five!"

Teddy watched Wally's delight as the woman was helped from the water. Wally was a fag and a jackass but he didn't think ole Walls would be involved in killing. What was it? What was he missing?

A flashing thought came to him! He knew, suddenly Teddy *knew* what was going on. He was watching them film a show! A show, a kind of stupid show where people were tricked into making idiots of themselves, that was it. Maybe even that web thing, *YouTube*, yeah! He hadn't witnessed a murder; he had seen them filming re-takes to get it right. Yes! Twenty-five takes! Jesus, God, thank you! Teddy was surprised to feel tears in his eyes, real tears. Tears of relief mingled with the salty ocean water stinging his eyes. Oh, God! He was the unwitting stooge of a dumber version of that old show his mother watched on Retro-TV every night. What was its name? Oh, yeah, *Candid Camera*. What he saw today was being filmed all for his benefit.

Walking over to the pool, Teddy sank down on a lounge chair. The heat was so strong his clothes had dried, and he was sweating again. Shit! A scam show! *That's* what that fuck Bernie was having them do to him! He was on some sicko show. He had to hand it to ol' Bernz. Who knew the drugged-out bastard even had the intelligence to think of having this practical joke pulled on him?

Teddy began thinking that they would have to do some editing on this show, though. He couldn't have them televise the part where Bello talked about Teddy cheating on his wife Cate. No way! Fuck that! He figured they had release forms he had to sign, after all, and he'd be damned if he'd sign one without having the show edited to his liking.

He looked out at the boat and saw that it was being rowed farther out to sea towards a little speck of an island. Probably have a sea-plane waiting for the actors. Zip them to their hotel to get ready for tomorrow's stooge. Actors! Well, they *had* convinced him that the woman was being drowned. Jeez!

Mr. Bello appeared, carrying two tennis rackets and an envelope, and walked over to Wallis. Teddy saw Wallis smile as Bello handed him the envelope. He heard Wallis say, "Yes, Sir. Twenty-five today. I said twenty-five, didn't I? Thank you, thank you."

Wally. Probably got paid a little extra for playing the hysterical homo. Man! Teddy sighed with relief and exhaustion. Too much emotion here. And he was hot, so hot. Probably had heat exhaustion too. Well, enough now. Time to get everything settled, tell them to send the release to his office at the university—he'd have his lawyer look it over before he signed of course. Time to get out of here, go home, and get out of these sticky clothes. He needed to get into a cool shower and a warm pussy in that order.

He thought of his wife, Cate. She must be really pissed that he hadn't called. He'd make it up to her, give her a bullshit story about having to get paperwork done. Take her out to dinner and then get *her* done, do her really good. Truth was that Cate was a sexy wild woman in bed, he didn't really need any other woman. It was time he broke it off with Mitzy anyway. He had a full professorship waiting for him. Time to be respectable. The respectable Professor Ted Jameson.

Mr. Bello was approaching him now. Teddy saw that he was smiling. This was a good time to let Mr. Tennis Whites know *he* knew what was up. Bello probably knew it too. After all, he had to know that Theodore Carter Hugh Jameson was no fool. Bernz must have told him that Teddy was one smart bastard. They'd had to drug him to get him here, hadn't they?

"Well, Mr. Jameson. I understand you played the hero today. Interesting. I shouldn't be surprised though. An athletic man like you. How are you feeling after your escapade?"

Teddy looked at Bello and thought he was probably the producer, the money man behind the show. A regular P.T. Barnum, a real artist when it came to making money, he'd bet his life on that one. He decided to be charming to Mr. Bello and compliment him on the act, *then* hit him with not signing the release until they'd edited the tape.

"They're good at this, Bello. Really had me going there for a while."

"They're *very* good at what they do, Mr. Jameson. It's an art that they've had time to perfect." Bello glanced at his Rolex.

"I mean, I really was convinced, you know? I really thought that woman was drowning. Scared me shitless, Bello."

"Yes? That's interesting." He smiled, with those blinding white teeth.

"Your actor, the woman, is she a stunt person?"

Mr. Bello appeared to seriously consider Teddy's question, then shook his head. "No, I don't believe she ever *was* a stuntwoman."

"No? Well, they were all good. Really good. Maybe they're going to be big names someday. Everybody starts out in small budget stuff. Look at soap opera actors. Some go on to great careers."

Mr. Bello discreetly yawned and lazily swung the rackets. "Willing to play that game of tennis yet, Mr. Jameson?"

Teddy watched the waves of heat shimmer in front of his eyes and studied the man in front of him. Mr. Bello had not one drop of sweat on his face or his arms and legs, while he, Teddy, felt as if his clothes were plastered to his sweaty skin. Time to stop being Mr. Charm and let Bello have it.

"I already told you I don't play tennis in the heat. I schedule my matches for the early mornings, nothing after 8:00 a.m. Anyway, the hell with tennis, I know what's going on and I know that, by law, I have to sign a release form before you can show any of the shit you filmed here today. Let's talk about that, okay?"

"Release form, Mr. Jameson?"

"Yes, a release form. You filmed me without my knowledge. You can't show any part of the film you took with me in it without my express permission." Teddy paused before continuing. "You basically drugged me, kidnapped me, and tried to make me believe I was dead and in Hell of all places. You then had actors put on a stupid play where I thought I saw a woman being murdered. You did all this for some ha-ha asshole show you produce for the viewing pleasure of mindless idiots. Did you advertise in one of those retarded graphic magazines that Bernie reads? He must've read that you were looking for innocent stooges to be scammed for your show and gave you my life history and where you could find me."

Teddy had to catch his breath. The hot air was making it hard to breathe. "You and Wally played your parts well. So did those pathetic-can't-get-a-real-acting-job amateurs. You—"

"She wasn't being murdered. She was being punished." Mr. Bello swung one racket in an expert backhand.

"Oh-ho you're good! Now you're trying to get me to believe more bullshit. Where's the camera? I'm not playing along with this. Where's the *fucking* camera?"

"There's no camera, Mr. Jameson. You simply saw a woman being endlessly punished. An everyday occurrence here."

22

"Look, don't even attempt —" He stopped. The air was burning his lungs. He looked at Bello, so damn cool. Didn't he feel the heat? Bello smiled at him.

"Help! Help me! No! No more, please, help me!"

Teddy spun around and saw a screaming man being chased by two larger men. One of them was carrying a bucket and the other had something small and silver in his hand. The screaming man was running towards Teddy and Mr. Bello. He tried to pass them, but as he came up to them, Mr. Bello lowered a tennis racket and thwacked the man in the legs, causing him to fall, sprawling in the sand.

"We got you. Again," said the man with the bucket. He threw he contents on the fallen man just as the other large goon reached them. The smell of gasoline filled the hot air.

"No, *please, please,* no, don't let them, please!"

The man appealed to Teddy and Bello. Teddy went to go to him but Mr. Bello grabbed him in an iron grip and said quite firmly, "Step back, Mr. Jameson. You are not allowed to interfere. Rules."

The man with the silver object in his hand stood over the begging man. Teddy saw with horror that the object was a lighter. The man looked at Bello and asked, "Now?" With a smile, Bello nodded yes. Carefully, almost reverently, the man with the lighter knelt down and flicked a flame to life, brought it close to the gasoline soaked clothes of the man on the sand, and lit them. The man erupted into a screaming, rolling ball of fire.

"Oh, my God! We've got to help him!" screamed Teddy struggling to free himself from Mr. Bello. "Cover him with sand, drag him into the surf—don't just stand there! Bello! What's wrong with you?!"

The man on fire rolled and rolled on the sand but the flames would not be extinguished. Teddy had never felt so helpless and so physically sick. He leaned to the side and vomited. He kept doing this until he had only dry heaves left. Then he hung in Bello's grip, exhausted. My God!

After the body stopped moving, the two beefy men walked over and kicked sand over the remains to cover the smoldering heap. The awful odor of burned flesh hung heavy in the still air. Mr. Bello let Teddy drop to the ground where he lay too shocked to even move.

"Scoop him up. You know where to bring him," said Mr. Bello. The men shoveled the burnt remains into the bucket and carried it away.

Teddy felt his mouth fill with bile. He had seen a horrible, unthinkable act of violence occur. What had the man done to deserve such a death? This had to be the work of a mob. Only organized crime took somebody out in this terrible way.

"Is everything all right, Mr. Jameson?"

Hearing Bello's quiet voice ask that question, anyone would think he was concerned for Teddy's feelings. As if he were a kind maitre d' asking

Teddy if the dinner at a pricey restaurant had been to his liking.

"You burned a man alive!" Teddy was on his feet now.

"Oh, hardly alive Mr. Jameson. Hardly."

"Are you fucking crazy, or am I? I just saw you give your *okay* for that poor man to be set on fire!"

"That you did, I'll grant you that, Mr. Jameson."

"*Why?!* Why would you give an order to do that? Why?" Teddy felt nauseous again.

"Rules. Yes, rules, Mr. Jameson."

"What rules, in the name of God, what damn rules would make you want to burn a man to death?"

"Oh," laughed Bello, "*that*. I didn't kill him, neither did my minions. No. You can't kill someone who's already dead. That is an *unbreakable* rule, Mr. Jameson."

"*Already* dead? He was alive! I saw him *running* and begging for help. You saw it too. He wasn't dead until your *minions,* as you call those knuckle-draggers, flame-broiled the poor bastard."

"Ah, no. Just punishment, that's all. Not murder. Murder is against the rules."

Teddy stared at Bello. This was insane. The man in tennis whites, casually practicing air shots with his racquet, looked completely calm and unnerved by what had just happened.

Maybe I *am* crazy or maybe I really am tripping on drugs, thought Teddy. This can't be *real*, it can't. But it isn't one of those stupid scam shows either. *That* man was burnt to a crisp. No way it was a stunt. There was nothing left of him! Someone is supposed to be left alive after a stunt, right? That's what stunts did. You *think* someone is killed or whatever, but, after the stunt, they get up and walk away. They don't crumble into ashes that are scooped up into a bucket!

"No, no! Please, no!"

Teddy turned and his heart slammed in his chest. The 'poor flame-broiled bastard' was running towards him again! It was unbelievable! Just as before, he was chased by those two goons, one carrying a bucket, the other a lighter. This time, instead of Bello whacking his legs to make him fall, the man tripped over his own two feet, landing about ten yards from where Teddy stood. Again the gasoline was poured on him, again he was set ablaze.

Teddy got up and tried to run to the man but found his legs wouldn't move fast enough. It was like one of those dreams where you're running from danger but can only run in slow motion. He sat down on the sand again, put his head in his hands and cried. Mr. Bello came over and sat next to him. He consulted his watch and gave a signal to one of the goons standing over what was left of the burning man. The man scooped sand over the fire until no flames were left. The one who had held the lighter again shoveled what remained into the bucket and they walked away.

Mr. Bello inhaled deeply and got to his feet. "Such a perfect day for tennis. Care for that game now, Mr. Jameson?"

Suddenly Teddy knew that he was dealing with an unbelievably dangerous man. Something was *so* wrong. He had no idea how he had gotten here, or even why he *was* here. The thought that Bernie O'Connell had had anything to do with this was no longer valid. Bernie was a drunk and a coke-head but he was also too stupid to think up something like this. There had to be another reason for this whole show.

He didn't feel that drugged. He wasn't crazy. There was a sinister reason for him being here. But what? Is it possible this is a kidnapping? Cate's parents were pretty well off—in fact, they were what you'd call wealthy. Cate's mother came from old money and ran an upscale boutique. Her father had an accounting firm. Was this a ransom deal? Cate had once told him that her mother had watched her like a hawk when she was a little girl for fear someone might kidnap her. People with money always feared that for their children, Cate said. But why take *him?* Unless they had also taken—

His blood seemed to freeze in spite of the intense heat. Oh God, did they have Catie somewhere here too? Bello had asked him if he knew how Cate was, hadn't he? Oh my God!

"Is my wife here?" Teddy asked bluntly facing Bello.

"Your *wife?* Now why would that good woman be *here* of all places? Now your whore—"

"Just fucking answer me, okay? Is Cate here or not?"

He sized up Bello, figuring that if he rushed him he could take him. Maybe not easily, but he'd still be able to punch his pretty boy face a few times before one of his people came to his rescue.

With a smile just touching his lips, Mr. Bello looked at Ted unflinchingly. "No, Mr. Jameson, no, your wife is not here."

Teddy stared at Bello and for some reason he couldn't explain, knew he was telling the truth. They didn't have Cate. But what the hell did they want with *him?* Did they think that his in-laws would actually *pay* money to get *him* back? His in-laws disliked him intensely. His father-in-law was so cheap where Teddy was concerned that he always nit-picked the bill whenever they met for lunch. No way would they consider any ransom demands for *him.*

Ted's mother didn't have any money except what Teddy sent her monthly. His father had left her nothing but her freedom for which both she and Teddy were grateful. He tried to think if he owed anybody any money. He wasn't a big gambler, just a few ball games when he felt lucky. No, the last time, a few years ago, when he had trouble paying a gambling debt, the neighborhood boss had sent a knuckle-breaker to threaten him and the threat was all it took for Teddy to come up with the cash fast. Since then, nope, no money owed anybody but the monthly payments to the mortgage company and *they* don't use physical force to get their payments.

It had to be blackmail about Mitzy. Scare tactics, yeah, ol' Bernie's whole fucking family had been in the IRA, that bunch of crazy micks. Bernzie wants money, that's all. He decided that he was just going to be blunt and confront Mr. Bello. If it *was* a kidnapping, he'd get no money no matter what he did to Teddy. He didn't even want to *think* about what they might do to him considering what he had just seen, but no matter, there would be no money. He closed his eyes.

But, wait, all this can't really be happening, something is so wrong, so wrong. People don't get burnt to death and rise up like the Phoenix. What am I missing? God, it is so fucking hot!

It was too quiet now. Opening his eyes, he looked around him and saw he was all alone. Where was Wallis, the old butler, the 'fire-men'? How did Bello leave without Ted hearing the crunch of the sand under his feet? His head felt strange, he saw things too sharply. He looked down at the sand and the crystals looked alive and moving ever so slightly. Maybe I *am* under the influence of some powerful drug or combination of drugs he thought. Something unknown on the street. His earlier bravado was fading. He was becoming afraid and he didn't like it.

If this was a hallucination, it was one for the medical books. Teddy had read that the poet, Samuel Taylor Coleridge had taken opium or some other mind drug, fallen asleep and had a dream which turned out to be the basis for the poem *Kubla Khan*. Coleridge had written down most of what he remembered when he awoke. Teddy had loved that imagery. Hell, maybe he would write *this* shit down and become famous! He laughed.

'In Xanadu did Kubla Khan,
a stately pleasure-dome decree,
Where Alph the sacred River ran,
in caverns measureless to man,
down to a sunless sea...'

Teddy turned with surprise at the voice reciting *Kubla Khan* and saw Bello walking towards him, carrying a heavy tennis bag.

"Magnificent poem isn't it? Rare and haunting. One of the most haunting poems that came from human mind. *'Caverns measureless to man...'*" He dropped the bag and looked out to the ocean. "Measureless, Mr. Jameson. Imagine what that means! Like time—imagine time without measure. Can you even fathom that concept?"

Teddy felt a spasm of fear. How did Bello know he was thinking of that poem? The fear threatened to intensify when he heard Bello laugh.

"Oh I know *everything*, Mr. Jameson. I've known every thought you've had since you arrived here. I know that you suspected your drunken friend Bernie of having something to do with your being here. And that you then believed that you were being filmed for one of those shows which make a horse's ass out of unsuspecting jerks like you. I also know that now you think you've been the victim of a kidnapping plot and that you're worried that no one will pay a ransom for your return." Mr. Bello stood there, tan, perfect, and with not a drop of sweat on his skin. "So you see, Mr. Jameson, I know every single thought that has gone through your mind, even the rather vulgar thought about getting into 'a cool shower and then a warm pussy' in reference to your lovely, lovely wife Catherine. I know it all."

Teddy felt his head begin to pound. Maybe he was crazy. He'd had an aunt who was confined to a mental hospital. She had once served her own shit as patè at a dinner party. It could run in the family. One thing for certain, though, if he didn't find out for sure what was going on he knew he'd *become* crazy. Stark raving mad crazy!

Mr. Bello laughed. "Oh, Mr. Jameson, that is good! Her own excrement? Very amusing. Tasty patè!" He laughed again. "But you're not crazy, sir, no, not at all. Actually it would be so much better for *you* if you *were* insane, but, sadly, you're not."

Teddy stood and spoke to the back of Bello's head. He didn't want to look into his eyes. He felt a little vulnerable and slightly afraid. Everything that had happened was too surreal, too otherworldly. It was not normal.

Bello sniffed the air and Teddy wondered if he was smelling Teddy's fear. Animals did that. Then some of Teddy's bravado returned. Everything had to have an explanation, even Bello's mind reading tricks.

"Mr. Bello? I'm asking you man to man here. Tell me what is going on. You said some strange things before about how I should know where I am—but I don't, I really don't. You asked if I had seen my uncle lately, but I think you know that he's been dead for over twelve years. I don't know what you mean. I've seen weird unbelievable things happen here and I can't figure out what is going on. I'm—" He took a ragged breath. "I've seen people die and then come alive. You keep talking about rules and how murder is against the rules, but I swear I do believe I've seen murder committed even though the people who die keep coming back! Tell me please, for God's sake, where the fuck I am, okay?" He took another breath. "I *want* to hear that we're in the Caribbean on some private island and this is all either a horrible, sadistic game being played for my benefit or I'm on a drug so powerful that my mind is tricked into thinking what I see is real." Pause. "Because it seems real—it seems nightmarishly true."

Teddy turned and watched the waves. With dripping sarcasm, he said to Bello, "This place. Mitzy calls places like this paradise. Yeah, it's beautiful and all, but it's *not* exactly paradise, is it Mr. Bello? It isn't—"

Bello sighed deeply and said very softly, almost sadly, "No, Mr.

Jameson, it is not. It isn't Paradise at all, not at all."

The sun was setting in a brilliance of red and gold. It looked like it was being swallowed up by the ocean itself. The gigantic fiery ball dipped beneath the horizon, disappearing into the water making the surface of it shimmer.

As Teddy and Bello watched, the ocean water seemed to boil as if the heat of the setting sun had settled in its hidden depths. The water roiled and bubbled like a huge pot waiting to be filled with food. It seemed alive. But there was no sign of life, nothing living could withstand that heat. No fish, no mammal, thought Teddy with detachment. Next to him he heard Bello utter a strange sound almost like a sigh, but deeper. More guttural.

Waves touching the shore no longer appeared to be lapping water but looked, instead, like live tongues of flame scorching the sand. The edge of the shore was turning a deep coral red. Somewhere there was the sound of a scream cut short, then somebody laughing.

Beyond the pool there was some noise and activity. Teddy looked over his shoulder. The sound of muted voices came to him and he could see figures moving. A sort of chanting began. Cries of "Lu-chee! Lu-chee!" were heard. The way it was being repeated over and over again sounded as if they were calling the name of someone who was famous, someone well-known and revered. Thunder rumbled overhead.

"Lu-chee! Lu-chee! Lu-chee!"

The chanting grew louder and louder. It was almost deafening. Mr. Bello turned towards the chanting sound and raised his arms high over his head.

"Lu-chee! Lu-chee! Lu-chee!" It was chanted with passion.

Lightning flashed onto the surface of the water. The tiny licks of flame made a halo around the shore's edge.

"Lu-chee! Lu-chee! Lu-chee!" Fervent, louder. Teddy covered his ears.

Mr. Bello brought his arms down and spread them wide to the sides in a gesture of an all-encompassing embrace. He looked like one of those old time evangelical preachers you would see in a movie about the old South.

Teddy stood riveted, watching Bello, mesmerized by the chanting, dizzied by the heat. *What*, he thought, is Lu-chee?

"Not *what*, Mr. Jameson, *who*."

"Who? I don't understand. Lu-chee? Who is Lu-chee?"

"I, Mr. Jameson, *I* am Luci, an endearment if you will, a shortened version of my full name, L-u-c-i-b-e-l-l-o. Lucibello, the Beautiful Light."

Teddy stared uncomprehendingly.

"Ah, Teddy, Teddy." Bello lowered his arms and clasped his hands in front of his chest. "It is an Italian word—Lucibello. It means Beautiful Light. Do you understand now? Do you know what it signifies, this name?" Teddy shook his head slowly. Lucibello sighed.

"It is the name of a specific ethereal being, a name that was once associated with the beauty of the celestial heights."

In spite of the unbearable heat, Teddy felt chills shudder through his body. He began to shake. It had to be a drug. He was convinced of that now. The crowd by the pool area had increased and the chanting was softer but still intense.

"This being," Bello continued, "this incredibly exquisite being was God's favorite, *His* finest creation. God was, to give you a human analogy, Lucibello's Michelangelo, and, in turn, Lucibello was His *David* and *Pietà* combined. The perfect, Beautiful Light of God."

Teddy wrapped his arms tightly around his chest to keep them from trembling uncontrollably. He was so hot yet his hands were like ice, his sweat was cold. Hot and cold at the same time—he'd heard of a street drug that had that same after-effect.

"What's the name of drug you gave me, you bastard?" His speech slurred. The perfect blue of Bello's eyes made contact with Teddy and he couldn't look away. They were like intense blue flames.

"*What* don't you comprehend, Ted? Surely you know by *now*. Beautiful Light, God's finest creation? His *favorite*—until the well-known Fall From Grace, of course." Bello smiled at Teddy's look of confusion. "You *know* who I am, don't you Ted? Oh, and Ted? You can call me Lu. I'm giving you permission to do that. We should be on a first name basis—now."

Teddy's legs could no longer support him and he sat down on the sand with a thud. Lucibello stood over him and Teddy saw the lean muscle mass of his calves and thighs. A tennis player's legs, he thought idiotically. That he could even think of that when he felt so sick and dizzy made Teddy give a sardonic laugh. This had to be some type of hypnosis or mind game combined with a powerful psychotic. Everything he saw had been a mind illusion—the drowning, the man set on fire, all hypnosis of some kind

"Join me at the feast, won't you Ted? We have prepared a sumptuous feast for you and the others."

Lu Bello extended a hand to Teddy to help him up. Teddy hesitated only briefly before accepting it and being hauled to his fest. He felt light-headed and weary.

Wallis came scurrying across the sand to where the two were standing. "We're ready, Sir. Everyone is awaiting your presence."

"And Charles?" Bello asked this in a low voice.

Wallis lowered his head. "He knows his place, Sir, knows what is expected of him." Under Bello's stare, he added, "And, of course, the *consequences* of any disobedience."

Bello looked at Teddy and gestured expansively towards the pool area. There were tables set up and the smell of rich, savory food being cooked wafted towards them.

"We'll take the long path. Let me show you around before we dine. Let me show you the— *good* life—if you will."

They walked slowly around the beach. People passing Mr. Bello inclined their heads in a polite bow. "I believe I have someone here who will be happy to clear the whole matter up for you, Ted. After dinner tonight he'll explain everything."

"And that would be your company lawyer?"

In spite of feeling like shit, Teddy spoke with the contemptuous assurance he tended to use when he felt he was not in control.

"Ah, no, Ted, he was never a lawyer. You should know that."

Teddy paused. "I *should* know this, *surely* I do know that. According to you I should know a lot about this place and people I've never met. Well, if you are so good at mind reading *you* already know that *I* have no fucking idea about anything here." He swayed slightly. "And I feel really sick; I think I might need a doctor. Whatever drug this is, I'm having a bad reaction here. That's funny too, because I felt fine before."

"A doctor is not what you need. All will be explained. You're just reacting to the heat and heated emotion."

Bello showed the property off like a true land baron. Even feeling as sick as he did, Teddy could see the beautifully landscaped gardens, the pristine paths of perfect shells leading down to the beach. He could admire the infinity pool that looked as if it had no end and the soft glow of the underwater lights at the pool's bottom. Teddy stopped, gazing at the glowing water of the pool.

"Maybe I should go for a swim. It's got to be cooler in the water than walking around. Isn't it supposed to cool down in the Caribbean at night? It's gotten hotter. I need a swim. I hate doing anything in the heat."

"You enjoy swimming, don't you Ted. You enjoy it immensely." It was a statement, not a question.

"Whoever told you that bit of info knows me pretty well. Enjoy it? Shit no, I *love* it. That's why when I get my full professorship, I'm having a huge pool installed in my backyard. A beautiful in-ground Olympic pool."

He started to head over to the pool but was quickly stopped by Bello. "I'm terribly sorry, but you can't use the pool, Ted."

"Why, is it being *cleaned?* Looks pretty sparkling to me." Teddy knew he sounded sarcastic but he was unbearably hot.

"You can't use it, Ted." Bello showed his perfect teeth in a perfect smile. "Ever."

Teddy was too woozy from the heat to argue. Forget swimming, he just wanted to get home. In the distance, beyond the pool area, Teddy could see the tennis courts. They looked way too bright, too lit up with what looked like shimmering shadows. The lights would make the courts hot, even at night.

He remembered the early morning game with his department chair tomorrow and closed his eyes. He didn't know what time it was but he guessed it had to be around nine o'clock. Oh, God, he had to get out of here!

In contrast to the brightly lit tennis courts the dining area was bathed in soft candlelight. There were strings of lights wrapped around, and hanging between, tall palm trees and other foliage, but they weren't turned on. Obviously Bello believed in dinner ambience, thought Teddy nastily. Large tables had been set up and the smell of food was almost overwhelming. Something to eat, nothing to drink but water, and then Teddy would try one more time to find out what this was all about. There had to be a reason—if he thought rationally he would figure it out. Economics, his teaching field of expertise, required rationality and he was an expert in his field.

When they approached the dining area, Wallis hurried over and showed Teddy to his table. There were seven very comfortable looking chairs and one that obviously was reserved for whoever would be sitting at the head of the table. Teddy looked around and saw all the tables were set up in the same way. The only difference was that the large chair at the head of *his* table was more ornate, almost like a special chair used for a throne. Like, he thought, that chair he'd once seen in a cathedral. He remembered that chair.

He'd been ten years old when his uncle Charlie had taken him to a Roman Catholic mass in a cathedral. He had pointed out the beautiful and intricately carved chair on the altar and said it was reserved for church royalty, the archbishops, the Princes of the Church.

Uncle Charlie, a recent Catholic convert, was in awe of the pageantry of his new religion. Teddy had been impressed with all the gold and Italian marble he had seen. His uncle had sworn him to secrecy.

"Don't tell anyone, Teddy," Uncle Charlie had said. "Your Dad won't like that I took you here."

But his father found out and had been pissed as anything that Charlie had taken his son to a 'Popish place of sin.' He was a strict born-again Christian who hated the Catholics. When Teddy defended his uncle and said he thought the cathedral was beautiful, his father had smacked him hard enough across the mouth to cause an ugly split lip. Teddy never forgot it or forgave his father. In his mind the chair and the split lip had been joined forever.

"Ah memories, hmmm, Ted? Interesting how they can haunt you." Bello spoke behind him. Wallis snickered at the comment and handed Teddy a glass of ice water. "Excuse me, Teddy. I must go change for dinner. Wallis will take care of you."

With great ceremony, Wallis held a chair out for Teddy to sit down.

"Where are the others, Wally? This is a table for eight."

In answer Wallis pointed in the direction of the beach. Teddy saw four people slowly making their way over the shell walkways towards them. He turned around to look for Bello but he was nowhere to be seen. He saw the old waiter hovering around one chair keeping his head down. He was dressed in a white dinner jacket that had seen better days.

As each person came to the table, Wally directed them to their place and gallantly held their chairs. When the four were seated, Wallis and the old waiter took their places at the table. Teddy could understand Wally sitting at the table but was a bit surprised that the old guy, the waiter, was allowed to sit with the guests.

The other tables were filling up and when everyone had been seated there seemed to be an air of expectancy. After a while, Teddy heard the murmur of "Lu-chee, Lu-chee," so low that it seemed to blend with the sound of the waves. Suddenly everyone rose as one.

"Please get *up*, Mr. Jameson, *get up!*" Wallis hissed in his direction.

Teddy got to his feet and saw Mr. Bello, resplendent in a white tuxedo coming back towards his table. On his way he nodded his head at the other tables and was greeted with murmured 'ahs' and clapping. At Teddy's table, Wallis rushed to help seat him and Bello smiled graciously at all assembled.

"Lucibello!" was reverently said by many voices, almost like a prayer. "Lucibello!"

Bello waved them to sit down and snapped his fingers. From an area behind the pool, servers began bringing platters of food. Some dishes deliciously cold, others steaming hot. The aromas were sweetly competing. Teddy found he was actually starving.

"Enjoy yourself, Ted," said Bello leaning towards him. "Eat all you want."

There were liquids to complement each dish; alcoholic as well as virgin drinks and ice water. Everyone was heaping their plates full as the servers presented the dishes to them. Everyone but the waiter.

"He can't eat anything," Bello whispered to Teddy, seeing him stare at the waiter.

"Stomach problems?" Teddy whispered back and Bello just smiled.

The food made Ted feel better, but he was careful to drink only ice water. Actually he felt very *much* better and quite alert. No tiredness, no queasiness, he felt nothing but good. That was to his benefit. He needed his wits about him for the *explanation* Bello had promised after dinner. Obviously he would be meeting with a lawyer and needing to sign a waiver.

The candlelight made everything look shadowy, but that was good. It made Teddy feel calm and relaxed. The food was superb, one of the best meals he had ever eaten. Bello was a charming host, a good conversationalist, talking about economics, Teddy's job, every day topics, but with an intelligence and flair that made it all fascinating. When everything was settled, Teddy had to find out if a person actually *could* vacation here. He laughed a little to himself. Good food, more than likely good liquor, and good conversation. Great place to come.

Wallis and Bello were deep in a whispered conversation and, pleasantly sated, Teddy looked around the table at his fellow diners. He was struck by something odd. Except for the old waiter, who sat with his hands folded in front of him, they were all eating and drinking. Nothing wrong there. But what was odd was that there was utter silence. There was a complete lack of conversation. No one was talking.

He squinted his eyes—everyone at his table was in shadow. He looked at people at other tables. There was no sound other than the clink of silverware on china. Strange. The silence was made complete because Wallis and Bello had stopped their conversation. They were looking at Teddy.

"Yes, Ted? Are you enjoying yourself? If you've quite finished dining, before they bring out the wonderful desserts, I have someone with whom you've been waiting to speak—someone who will explain why you have been brought here."

Now comes the legal bullshit, thought Teddy. Thank God, I didn't drink anything. Where is 'Mr. Lawyer?' As soon as Ted thought the question, he saw Bello nod pointedly to the old waiter.

"Ahem," the old man coughed as he slowly got to his feet. Teddy thought that the old guy was being told to go get the lawyer and so was surprised when he just stood waiting. He was more than surprised when he heard, "Hello, Teddy, my boy."

He stared at the old waiter. His voice! He sounded exactly like Teddy's beloved Uncle Charlie! This is impossible. Who was doing this? Teddy sat frozen in his seat as the lights in the trees slowly came on. The old waiter stood there with a sad smile on his face and then walked towards him.

"Teddy, oh Teddy, I *have* missed you, my beloved nephew."

The face was, without a doubt, that of Charles Jameson. Younger brother of Carter Jameson, beloved uncle of Ted Jameson, looking exactly the same as the last time Teddy had seen him alive when they'd had what was to be their last dinner together. Exactly as he must have looked right before he was struck and killed by a bus while crossing a local street on his way to confession.

"Uncle—*Charlie?!*"

The old man nodded and stopped in front of Ted's chair. "It's me, Teddy. I've missed you more than anyone else.

"But, you're— *dead!* I mean whoever you are, you're *not* my uncle because *he's* dead. Who the hell are you? What kind of insane joke is this?"

Teddy felt as if someone had punched the air out of him. His lungs burned. The lights were growing brighter.

"No, no, Teddy! It's really me. It's me, my boy!"

The man standing just inches from Teddy looked like Uncle Charlie but Teddy knew he wasn't, couldn't be. My God, I am crazy! Teddy turned to Bello with his lips curled in a snarl. Adrenaline pumped through him and he felt a killing rage.

"You mother-fucking sick, sick bastard! How could you *do* this? You made some actor look like my Uncle Charlie and thought it would be *funny*?! I should kill you!"

There was a collective gasp from the crowd of people. Bello was looking at Teddy and this time there was no smile on his face. He looked fearless, commanding and completely in charge—like royalty, untouchable, his rule unquestioned. He looked cruel.

"*You* are hardly in a position to do *anyone* any harm, Ted, least of all *me*. Who do you think you are? Do you think you're GOD?" Bello said the last word with intense viciousness.

"I don't know why I'm here. I am assuming it has to do with some type of blackmail. This is too much for a simple joke. Tell me—"

"Kirk cheated on the Kobayashi Maru, Teddy. Remember?"

Teddy stopped and stared at the fake Uncle Charlie. He couldn't breathe. "*What* did you say?!"

"I said, Kirk cheated on the Kobayashi Maru!"

The old waiter smiled broadly at Teddy. Teddy was stunned. *Nobody* but Uncle Charlie would know what that phrase meant to Teddy. It was their code, their secret. The phrase itself had to do with Teddy's and Uncle Charlie's favorite *Star Trek* movie.

In the movie a new Starfleet officer is in awe of James T. Kirk because Kirk was the only cadet who had ever passed a test called the Kobayashi Maru at Starfleet Academy. The test pit man against computer, putting the cadets into an un-winnable situation. No one had ever beaten the computer because it was programmed so that only the machine could win.

But, the night before taking the test, Kirk had snuck into the area where the test was given and surreptitiously re-programmed the computer simulator so that *he* had a chance of winning. He out-witted and beat the computer. When confronted by his superiors at Starfleet Command for what they termed was cheating, he justifies his actions by arguing that putting cadets in a no-win situation is *in itself* cheating. Starfleet is so impressed by his rationale that they award Kirk a commendation for superior thinking.

Teddy remembered Uncle Charlie saying that what Kirk did was for the ultimate good, a sort of 'the ends justify the means' thinking. That type of thinking helped Teddy make a crucial decision in his senior year of high school, a decision only Uncle Charlie ever knew about.

Senior year, Teddy's main problem was money—there was not enough of it for him to go on to college. The money saved from his part-time jobs was nowhere near what he would need even for a half year. He needed a money miracle. In April of that year, he seemed to get a chance at that miracle.

The wealthy owner of a local real-estate company was offering a full four-year scholarship to Stanford for qualified students. Teddy's grades were excellent and he was only one of two seniors to apply for it. But the other applicant presented a major problem. That senior had an advantage over Teddy with her higher GPA. Teddy felt frustrated and desperate.

It wouldn't be fair if she won because, while her parents could well afford to send their daughter to any school she chose, Teddy knew his chances of getting a quality education depended solely on that scholarship. It could change his whole life. In order to win, Teddy, like the fictitious Kirk decided to take matters into his own hands. The day after the two application letters were submitted to the senior counselor, he did just that.

All scholarship application letters were kept in the guidance office. He knew the guidance secretary left the office twice in the morning. Once at nine-thirty for her twenty-minute morning break, during which time she locked the door. The second time was her bathroom run at eleven, when she *didn't* lock it. He had only that ten-minute window at eleven to do what he needed to do and he had to be fast.

His phys.ed. class was down the hall from guidance.
Leaving his class on the pretext of getting a drink of water, he watched as the secretary walked swiftly down the hall to the ladies' room. Making sure no one was around, he went into the office, rifled through the outgoing mail and stole his competitor's application. He went home and burned it.

Two months later, when Teddy was awarded the scholarship, he confessed what he had done to Charlie and wondered if it was right to accept it. His uncle told him to take the scholarship and never tell anyone else about how he got it.

"This is a great opportunity, my boy. You did what you had to do to get into that school. The ends justify the means here. You'll do more with that education than that other kid would have done." Then he winked at Teddy and, referring to the *Star Trek* movie, had said, "Kirk cheated on the Kobayashi Maru."

Now Teddy stared at the old waiter. "Oh my God, you *are* Uncle Charlie! How or why doesn't matter, you're alive! Uncle Charlie!"

Teddy was up on his feet and embracing the old man, almost knocking him over. His uncle was crying.

"My boy, my boy!"

"I don't know what the hell is going on here Uncle Charlie! You were dead, I *saw* you dead in the hospital! How can this be? Oh hell, I don't care how you came to be here, I'm just so happy that you're here!"

Uncle Charlie sat down next to Teddy who was blubbering like a baby and held him close. The lights in the trees were illuminating everything around them.

"You were dead, now you're alive, you're alive!" Teddy couldn't stop saying that. "Oh, you're alive!"

"Charles, I believe you have something to say to your nephew Ted." Bello's voice was strong and commanding. "Something important. Now."

Charles let Teddy go and sat up straight. He was shaking.

"What's the matter, Uncle Charlie? What do you have to say to me? We could always tell each other everything, you and me. Did you somehow fake your own death to get away from somebody? I know how you took money from Aunt Lillian to play the horses. Did she find out? Is that it? I won't tell anyone. What is it?"

Charles Jameson put his head in his hands for a minute and then, sighing, looked up at his nephew.

"My dear, dear boy. Teddy. I am not what you think I am. I am not what you call—alive. I really *am* dead."

Teddy said nothing, just stared at his uncle. "*Dead?* That's impossible. You're here talking to me. Do you mean dead inside, like you're afraid to come back home? I'll help you, honest, Uncle Charlie. I'll do anything for you, I'm so glad you're alive, here with me!"

Uncle Charlie sighed and tears streamed from his eyes. "Ah Teddy, Teddy! We're all dead here, my boy."

Teddy was trying to grasp something but it eluded him. Dead? His uncle had felt solid enough when he had embraced him. A flash of annoyance at his uncle rushed through him. He was too tired for any further crap.

"C'mon, Uncle Charlie! Stop fooling around. You're as dead as *I* am!"

Silence. Wallis giggled softly in the background.

"Uncle Charlie? I said you're as dead as *I* am, did you hear me? You're as *dead* as —"

Charles straightened up again and looked levelly at his nephew. His eyes, always so full of laughter, looked cold and sad. "Yes, Teddy, yes I heard you, and yes, you're right. I *am* as dead as you are."

"Dead? I'm not dead! What are you saying?" He stared at Charlie in disbelief. His uncle turned away.

The other guests at the table began to get up. While Teddy was still staring at his uncle, they walked up to where he was and waited in line. Bello stood up and tapped his shoulder.

"Why, look who's here Ted. Your fellow diners! I believe you know them all, every single one."

Though he spoke in a jovial manner, Bello had the look of a sadistic prison guard. He gave a signal and one by one the other guests began to greet Teddy.

"Hi Ted."

Teddy stared. He recognized the woman. She had been a childhood friend. Laurie Mendel. They'd lost touch.

"Hello Teddy," said a high-pitched voice. It was Burt Walmsey, a local accountant who used to do taxes for Ted's parents.

"Hey, Teddy, how's the man?" The powerful voice of Doctor Powers, his childhood doctor—he'd brought Teddy into the world.

And finally a voice that brought him back to a musty smelling, stuffy junior high classroom. The voice of Miss Pritchard. "Theodore Jameson, how are you?"

Teddy stared at the woman he hadn't seen since he was thirteen. In spite of the intense heat, she was wearing a heavy coat, and gloves. She stood shivering in front of him. "Miss Pritchard?" he whispered.

Bello leaned towards Teddy. "Ah, yes, Ted. You remember Miss Pritchard don't you, Summerhill Junior High School class of—"

Teddy stared at the woman who had been his eighth grade English Lit teacher. What was *she* doing here? He and his friends had always joked that she never took a vacation, that she lived in that moldy old school. What's the connection? And, Jesus, why was she wearing a coat?! It had to be over a hundred degrees here!

Bello beamed at him. He was enjoying the reunion.

"Miss Pritchard always hated the cold, didn't she, Ted? Remember when you and your friends were sweltering in her room and you begged her to let you open a window? She always said no, didn't she Ted? She never let you open a window, no matter how hot you were. Hated the cold then and hates it still. Ah, but she'll *never* get warm. Never."

All these people stood, just a bit ill at ease, near Teddy. Uncle Charlie came over and put his arm around his nephew.

"What's the connection here Uncle Charlie? Why are these people here? I mean how weird is it that people from my past show up all together? And I didn't think that ol' Doc Powers was still alive. I mean I heard that he was—." Teddy stopped.

"Yes, my boy?"

Teddy suddenly couldn't speak, couldn't move.

"What did you hear, my boy? That Doc Powers was dead? You can say it. He *is* dead, we're all dead.

Teddy looked at Dr. Powers who nodded his head in agreement.

"*All* of us here are dead." Uncle Charlie patted Teddy's shoulder. "You too, Teddy," he added softly.

"If I'm dead, how can I still move, how can I still think and talk." Teddy drew a ragged breath. "How can I breathe? I can't be dead. I have that tennis game tomorrow. I'm getting a full professorship!"

"Ah, tennis." Bello laughed.

Teddy grabbed his uncle by the arm. "Where am I Uncle Charlie? Please tell me where I am. No one will tell me anything but asinine hints like I *should* know exactly where I am, but I don't, Uncle Charlie, I don't! Where the *hell* am I?"

Charlie sighed, looked out towards the beach, and closed his eyes.

"You my boy, my dear, dear boy, *are* in Hell."

BROKEN RULES AND CONSEQUENCES

T eddy watched the clouds drift lazily over the starry sky and was only slightly aware of the music playing in the background. He didn't know the time; he didn't know how long he had been sitting on the beach. He only knew that Uncle Charlie, with the help of Mr. Bello, had explained everything that Teddy needed to know.

He knew the facts now. He was in fact dead and he was indeed in Hell. That Hell was as different as he could ever have imagined was still a problem for him. His father had made him believe Hell was all fire and brimstone and not a tropical resort where people ate and drank and the Devil acted, for the most part, as a munificent host.

Their punishments are all unique too. There is the fear and hate punishment—anything a person feared or hated is what they endured for eternity. The drowning woman for example, had hated being near water and feared drowning, the 'burning man' had always feared fire. Then there's the love punishment. Anything, or anyone, someone loved is within easy reach, but they can never, ever have it. There are horrible consequences for any disobedience.

"Oh, the punishments are diversified and tailored to each individual," laughed the Devil. "Oh yes. Look at poor Miss Pritchard. Condemned to be forever cold in the hottest place ever! Bitch!"

And it had also been explained that there were many different ways in which a person came to be in Hell. You didn't have to have been a Hitler, a pedophile, a mass murderer, or a rapist. It was all much more complex. People who had lived relatively good lives could be sent to Hell on a *technicality* all due to their particular religions. Real bastards, cruel, nasty, hateful bastards who followed all the rules of their faiths, went to Heaven.

Mr. Bello had been very nice in explaining about technicalities and the myriad ways people came to Hell because of them. He had begun with the people at Teddy's table and detailed how they came to be in Hell. All of the reasons had to do with religions. Lucibello had a cadre of lawyers working day and night finding loopholes and technicalities involving 'rule breakers'.

"Let's talk about religion, shall we Ted? Interesting topic, religion. There are so many, many rules in all of them. Break even one and it could spell disaster. Laurie Mendel, for example. Raised in a strict, orthodox Jewish family, her father a Rabbi, her mother keeping a kosher home. Laurie had disgraced her family by refuting Judaism which she called 'male-dominated bullshit.' She had even questioned the existence of God. Imagine! And believe me, God does exist. *That* is an irrefutable fact. *I* should know.

"She broke one of the Ten Commandants, you know, 'Honor thy father and thy mother?'" Bello became thoughtful. "If only she had *replaced* Judaism with another belief, that would have saved her. Many people do that, you know. Switch religions." He laughed. "It's all based on rules and technicalities. If she had become, let's say, a Christian or Buddhist and had embraced *those* beliefs whole-heartedly, well, she wouldn't be here now. But she broke the rules of her own religion and here she is condemned." He sighed happily.

"Burt Walmsey, now Burt was a good man, but he was gay. He had fought against his true nature all his life. In his forties, he met a man with whom he had found love and happiness. But..." Here Bello paused to snicker over the implied word 'butt,' "his Mormon faith was completely against sodomy. Did you know that the Church had even tried to *cure* him when he was a teenage boy by trying to force him to go to a bishop schooled in helping what they term degenerates? Burt refused to listen to them. No dice. It wouldn't have worked anyway, it never does." Bello laughed again. "Anyway, when Burt died in the arms of his lover, he was sent here. Rules you see, must be obeyed."

Teddy leaned forward. "What about Doctor Powers and Miss Pritchard? What could *they* have possibly done to get sent here?"

"Ah, interesting stories, those two." Bello sat back, obviously relishing telling his stories. "Dear Miss Pritchard became pregnant. She was so happy! She had accumulated quite a nice savings from all her years of teaching little shits like you and your friends. When she found out she was knocked up, she decided to leave her job, move away to a smaller, friendlier town and raise the child as a single parent. There was only one tiny little glitch."

He gave a dramatic pause. "During a routine test for chromosomal abnormalities, it was discovered that the child she was carrying was severely mongoloid. She knew that she could not raise a child like that alone and went to see the father of the child. He was a rather mean, self-centered man, but obviously a very good fuck. Anyway, Miss P. told him that she needed his help. He, wonderful father material that he was, told her 'it' was her problem and not to bother him again if she wanted to keep her teeth in her mouth. She really had no choice but to have an abortion. Went completely against her Catholic upbringing of course. The Catholics are tough on that—the good fathers believe that controlling a woman's body keeps her in her place. And, as the priest said to her after her confession, 'God loves you, dear, but yes, you *are* going to Hell.' Funny oh so funny! Loves you but it's Hell's that's awaitin' *you*, honey!"

Teddy looked at Lucibello standing there cool and relaxed, smiling as if he were recounting an amusing tale at a ritzy cocktail party.

"And Dr. Powers?"

"Oh, yes. Kindly Dr. Powers. Compassionate man, honest man, truly felt for his patients. *He* committed murder."

"Dr. Powers?! I don't believe it," said Teddy, suddenly incensed by what he was hearing. Dr. Powers had set his arm after Teddy fell out of a tree when he was thirteen. He'd been so kind, had even kicked Teddy's father out of the room when that cruel man demanded Teddy stop sniveling about the pain and be a man. Dr. Powers then told Teddy it was okay to cry, that a real man cries too. He made Teddy feel normal.

"Believe it, Teddy. It happened. He committed murder."

"No! Not him. He's a gentle, good man. He'd never kill anyone!"

"He would, he did. An Alzheimer patient to be exact. Do you know about Alzheimer's Teddy? The disease is a thief, it robs you of everything, your mind, your dignity, your very self. At the end, your brain can't even tell your lungs to breathe or your throat to swallow. Well, this poor patient of his could hardly breathe, every day was torture for her."

Teddy interrupted, "If he euthanized someone suffering from Alzheimer's that's more mercy than murder. That's not a sin."

"You'd *think* so wouldn't you?" replied Bello not at all put out by Teddy's interruption. "But, no, not according to the rules of the Lutheran Church—he was a Lutheran, you know. No mercy killings there, boy. Let the poor woman piss and shit herself while she's gasping for breath! Suffering is the only way to get to heaven, ha-ha. Suffering buys you a ticket to Paradise!" Bello looked suddenly angry.

"Anyway, he's standing over her bed, ol' Doc is. It reeks of wet shit and fresh urine. He's getting ready to listen to her heart, when, suddenly, she looks right at him and in a last moment of lucidity begs him to 'Please, have mercy, let me die, please, help me.' Then she begins gasping for breath again. The woman's husband is there with tears streaming down his face. He looks at Powers and asks him, 'Can't you help her, Doc'?

"The good doctor knows this can go on for a long while, her suffering and struggling to breathe, a lovely form of torture, so he gently holds her hand and tells her he will indeed, help her. He injects her with an overdose of morphine and continues holding her hand until the end. The husband doesn't say a word, just kisses the doctor's other hand and then embraces his wife." Bello sighs.

"Good man Dr. Powers, too bad he wasn't an atheist, he would be in heaven right this minute! The woman's husband knew it was a mercy, but the rules of Powers's religion say otherwise. 'Thou shalt not kill.' But that commandant was never meant to stop mercy-killing. Even the Devil knows that fact! Any other questions? I suppose you want to know how Charlie came to be here, yes?"

"Uncle Charles shouldn't be here. He doesn't deserve to be in Hell. My damn father should be here, that rotten fire and brimstone Bible-twisting bastard. *He* deserves Hell, not Uncle Charlie.

"Oh, Ted, Ted, I completely agree with you. But your father is singing with the angels! He went to church every Sunday, made sure to tithe 10% of all he had, and read the Bible every day. He was a righteous man, a cruel and a mean bastard to his wife and son, yes, but, in the eyes of his religion a thoroughly righteous man. *He* obeyed the *rules*. There are so many rules to be considered. We need a special book to keep track of them all. And sometimes, the rules change, God doesn't change them, only humanity. So some people who really *ought* to be in Heaven are here and some people who are here ought to be—well, you get the picture. I do try to make *certain* accommodations. I mean I am sensitive to a degree, but still, rules are rules. Break them and pay the piper."

Teddy stared straight ahead. "I can't see Uncle Charlie breaking any rules."

Bello paused, took off his Rolex, and smiled at Teddy.
"Charlie went to hell because he ate meat on Friday."

"That's bullshit! The Catholics did away with that regulation years ago!"

"Yes, yes they did, but, unfortunately, your uncle committed the sin *before* the rule was changed. He completely forgot about his sin, so to speak and, between you and me, he never was one who went regularly to confession. But Charles was a good man, I will admit. It was particularly unfair that, years later *on his way* to confession, he got hit by a bus. And the irony of it all is that, if he hadn't converted to Catholicism when he married your Aunt Lillian, he wouldn't be here. Go figure!" Bello sighed deeply.

"What's Charlie's punishment. Being a waiter?" Teddy couldn't help his sarcasm.

"No, his punishment is that he can never eat anything again. You know how much he loved to eat! Well that pleasure is gone. He can serve the food, he most certainly smells it, but he is not allowed to eat one morsel."

"And if he does?"

"Oh very simple. He gets cooked alive, like a lobster and eaten over and over again. So far he's been—good."

Lucibello stood and stretched. "Yes, people come here through all kinds of misunderstandings and technicalities. Very few come here by the traditional method of selling their soul to the Devil. That's so old hat! Modern society doesn't really believe that's possible any more. Still, there are some who try that bargain. Take

Wallis for example. You may have noticed it, gambling problem.

He sold his soul to me, to become one of the best and wealthiest gamblers in the world. He did quite well, too. I also made him very good-looking. He really was one of God's *ugliest* creations."

Bello shuddered dramatically.

"However, before he died, he tried to weasel out of the deal by offering to gamble with the Devil, winner take all! *Guess* who won? Now he's a trusted minion even though he still places too many bets here. I let him do it, keeps him contented and he is a hard worker. Ah, well—" He smiled. "I'll be going now Ted. A new guest will be arriving. This is an interesting one. I'm getting OJ himself! Imagine! Oh, before I forget, here, you'll need this. Don't want to be late now Teddy."

Bello places the Rolex in Teddy's hand, points to the heavy tennis bag near Teddy, smiles kindly, and turns to go.

"Is there anything I can do for you? You look so down. Want to see me vanish in a puff of sulfuric smoke? That always seems to cheer my guests up. No? Well then, see you tomorrow, noon sharp."

The kindness disappears and he says sadistically. "Do *not* be late, Mr. Jameson, there will be very unpleasant consequences if you are, I can assure you."

And he is gone leaving Teddy holding the gleaming new Rolex.

PUNISHMENT—TENNIS IN HELL

This *is* Hell, the *real* Hell, the place about which most of us have been warned at one time or another. I'm here on a technicality. I committed adultery and, according to the Catholic Church, that's a mortal sin. It is really Uncle Charlie's fault in a way. He had me baptized Catholic after my father died. Even though I never practiced it, I'm still subject to their rules. As Bello explained to me, the Catholics and the Orthodox Jews give him *quite* a lot of business with their laws, rules, and everything else.

As for me, well, I have a tennis match tomorrow at noon. I'll be playing tennis every day during the hottest part of the day, in the blistering heat, on a hot, hard clay court with no shade. Mr. Bello is being more than generous he says. He is so happy to play against someone of my, as he calls it, 'high caliber.' Even though I hate playing in the heat the alternative to being Bello's 'play mate' is certainly a Helluva lot worse.

If I even dare to miss even one match, I will have to be punished for my sin of adultery. It seems there is a special punishment reserved for male adulterers that dates back centuries, back to the time of the Borgia family, to be exact. Mr. Bello didn't want to tell me all the details but he did say that the punishment involved a roaring fire, a hot blade, my genitalia, and unbelievable pain.

"Wonderfully inventive torturers, the Borgias. My kind of sinners!" Lucibello had said with a satisfied smile.

Believe me I really didn't need to hear anything more. And since this is Hell, that punishment would be meted out to me again and again and again for *all* eternity.

Of course this will only happen to me *if* I miss a match, Mr. Bello was quick to assure me.

Only if I miss a match.

I don't plan to miss *any* matches in this God-forsaken place, that's for sure. Not a one.

For *all* eternity.

ABOUT THE AUTHOR

Kristen Houghton is the author of nine novels, two non-fiction books, a collection of short stories, and a YA novel. Her best-selling series, *A Cate Harlow Private Investigation,* has been voted one of the top five best new series of 2018 by the International Mystery Writers Association. Currently she is hard at work on a new YA series that features a paranormal investigator with distinct, untried powers of her own.

Kristen is a contributor to *The Horror Zine Magazine* and her horror stories have also appeared in anthologies.

Kristen Houghton is available for select readings and lectures. To inquire about a possible appearance, please contact Skylight-NYC Publishers at skylight-nyc@outlook.com Write Kristen Houghton in the subject line. For the latest new book by Kristen Houghton go to www.kristenhoughton.com.

www.ingramcontent.com/pod-product-compliance
Lightning Source LLC
Chambersburg PA
CBHW020607130626
46552CB00007B/3087